Based on the Mowgli Stories in *The Jungle Book*
and *The Second Jungle Book* by Rudyard Kipling.
Published by Hachette Partworks Ltd.
ISBN: 978-1-908648-64-8
Date of Printing: April 2013
Printed in Malaysia by Tien Wah Press

MOWGLI AND THE LOST ELEPHANT CHILD

Disney

H hachette

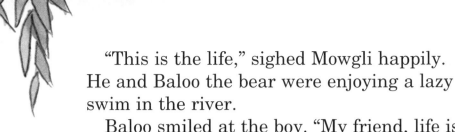

"This is the life," sighed Mowgli happily. He and Baloo the bear were enjoying a lazy swim in the river.

Baloo smiled at the boy. "My friend, life is too short to spend it worrying. Do the things you enjoy and be happy!" he declared.

Bagheera the panther looked down disapprovingly from a branch.

"What a pair of lazybones!" he exclaimed.

Bagheera
knew that
life in the
jungle was not
always easy.

Just then, the panther's ears twitched.
"Out of the water, you two!" he ordered.
"I can hear the sound of
trumpeting. Colonel Hathi
and his troop are on
their way –
and it sounds
as if they are
in trouble!"

"I hear them too," said Baloo. "I wonder what's happened? Elephants hardly ever need help, so it must be serious. Come on, Mowgli."

Baloo hoisted Mowgli onto his shoulders and waded out of the river.

The three friends hurried along the jungle path.
"Maybe we'll have to fight," said Baloo. "Well,
I'm not scared of anyone!" To prove it, he put up
his fists and started to box an invisible enemy.
"Anybody who wants to harm the elephants will
have to deal with me first!" he boasted.

At last, Mowgli and his friends arrived at a clearing. The elephants were all gathered round their chief, Hathi.

One of the elephants seemed especially upset.
"What's the matter?" Mowgli asked her.

"My little baby has disappeared!" she explained.
"He must have wandered off while I was having
a nap. I've been calling him for hours, but I can't
find him anywhere!"

"Don't worry," said Baloo kindly. "We'll help you
find him. He can't have gone far!"

Baloo, Bagheera and the elephants discussed the best way to organise the search for the lost calf.

But Mowgli was impatient. "Why waste time talking when we could be searching?" he said.

And so Mowgli set off to search alone.

Mowgli was an excellent tracker and soon, he discovered a clue.

"These are a man's footprints," he said. "I think I know what happened. This man has captured the elephant child!"

Mowgli was too busy following the tracks to notice that his enemy, Kaa the snake, was watching him.

"I sssspy a good ssssupper," hissed Kaa. "It's not often that Mowgli is alone. I musssst act fasssst!" He slithered after the boy.

But Kaa did not notice that he was being watched, too – by Shere Khan, the tiger!

    Shere Khan crept silently out of the long grass... and pounced on the python!

    "Sorry Kaa, old chum," he smirked. "But Mowgli is going to be MY supper!"

    "Ouch! You're squashing me!" complained Kaa.

Kaa did not like to argue with tigers. He slithered away.

"OK, you win this time," he muttered. "But I'm as hungry as a wolf, and I'm going to get that Mowgli sooner or later!"

Up ahead, Mowgli followed the tracks through the thick jungle. He didn't realise that he was being tracked too – by a hungry tiger!

Suddenly, Mowgli heard a
faint crying sound.

"I wonder where that noise is
coming from?" he said. The brave
little boy climbed up the nearest
tree to get a better view.

Mowgli clambered up a vine until he found a good lookout post on a high branch. He could see a clearing filled with cages of captured animals! A huge lorry was parked nearby.

"I'll wait until dark," decided Mowgli. "Then I'll sneak over and investigate."

As soon as night fell, Mowgli climbed down from the tree. By the light of the moon, he crept towards the camp.

"I must be as quiet as a mouse," he said. "Or I'll wake the guards!"

Just then, the baby elephant spotted Mowgli. He reared up his little trunk, ready to trumpet a welcome to his friend.

"Shh!" whispered Mowgli, pinching the end of the little elephant's trunk.

Mowgli quickly untied the rope around the
baby elephant's leg. As the elephant ran off to
find his mother, Mowgli silently crept over
to the animal cages.

One by one, Mowgli opened the cage doors and freed the animals.

Soon, there was just one more cage left to open. It contained a troop of very excitable monkeys.

As soon as Mowgli
let the monkeys out,
they whooped and
danced with joy.

Oh no! The racket
woke the sleeping
guards, and a light
went on in their tent.

"Run, monkeys!"
cried Mowgli.

The monkeys scattered and headed for the jungle. In no time, they were swinging from the branches high in the treetops, safe from danger. Mowgli headed for the river, closely followed by the animal thieves.

"Come back here, brat!" they yelled.

Mowgli reached the river bank. He spotted a floating log, leapt onto it and steered it into the middle of the river.

The thieves, stranded on the bank, were furious.

"That pesky kid!" they shouted. "He's freed all the animals and lost us a fortune!"

Mowgli, sitting on his tree-trunk boat, was enjoying himself. Using a fallen branch as an oar, he sang as he rowed along the river;
"One stroke on the left!
One stroke on the right!"
Mowgli didn't realise that he wasn't alone. On one bank of the river was a hungry snake with a rumbly tummy, and on the other was Shere Khan, who was every bit as hungry as Kaa!

Meanwhile, back in the jungle clearing, the
mother elephant suddenly let out a joyful trumpet.
"My baby!" she cried. "He's back!"

"Where have you been, darling?" asked the mother elephant. "We've been looking for you everywhere!"

"I was captured by some men who tied me to a post," explained the baby elephant. "But then Mowgli came and rescued me!"

"Mowgli?" exclaimed Bagheera. "I can't leave him alone for a minute! We must go and find him. He might be in danger!"

"Forward... MARCH!" commanded Colonel Hathi. "There's no time to lose to save Mowgli!"

The troop of elephants set off, the ground shaking as they pounded along the jungle path.

On the road, Bagheera met
the chattering monkeys.

"Are you looking for
Mowgli?" they asked the
panther. "He escaped from
the bad men by paddling a
log down the river."

"The river? Oh,
NO!" exclaimed
Bagheera. "The river
leads straight to the
waterfall!"

Mowgli didn't know he was in danger. He lay
back on the tree trunk, trailing his hand in the
water and daydreaming. He didn't notice the
quickening current and the rumbling noise as
the log neared the waterfall. In fact, Mowgli was
so relaxed that he fell asleep!

All of a sudden,
Mowgli woke with
a start. His log
boat seemed to be
travelling very fast!

"Mowgli saved us – now it's our turn to save him," said the monkeys. "We'll wait in this tree, which overhangs the river. When Mowgli passes, we'll grab him and pull him up to safety."

The monkeys waited. Then, just as Mowgli's log was about to topple over the edge of the waterfall, one of them grabbed him by the foot. Phew! Just in time!

The monkeys formed a chain and passed Mowgli
from one to the other. Then they tossed him to
Hathi, who caught the boy neatly with his trunk.

At last, Mowgli was safe!

Mowgli and his friends made their way back to the jungle clearing.

"Hooray for Mowgli!" trumpeted the elephants. "He brought us back our dear little lost baby!"

"You're so smart, Mowgli!" chattered the monkeys. "You saved us all from ending up in the zoo!"

"Well done, boy!" said Bagheera. "You have a kind and brave heart."

"And now it's time for a rest," added Baloo. "You must be exhausted!"

His jungle friends waved goodbye.

"Thank you, Mowgli! See you soon!"